For my mum, because lots of my favourite Scottish stories
are from the Borders and Skye. – *LD*

For PG and our travels here and there, all those years ago. – *CJ*

JANETTA OTTER-BARRY BOOKS

First published in Great Britain in 2013 and in the USA in 2014 by
Frances Lincoln Limited,
74-77 White Lion Street, London N1 9PF
www.franceslincoln.com

British Library Cataloguing in Publication Data available on request

ISBN 978-1-84780-342-9

Illustrated with digital collage

Set in Minion Pro

Printed and bound in China

1 3 5 7 9 8 6 4 2

Breaking the Spell

STORIES OF MAGIC AND MYSTERY FROM SCOTLAND

Written by **Lari Don**

Illustrated by **Cate James**

F

FRANCES LINCOLN
CHILDREN'S BOOKS

Contents

The Selkie's Toes

All around Scotland's coasts and islands, stories are told of selkies – seals who can shed their skins and turn into people.

Once upon a time, a fisherman fell in love with a selkie. He hid the selkie's sealskin so she would have to stay on land with him, and over time she grew to love him, and they had a little girl. But the fisherman knew that selkie stories hardly ever have happy endings, and he knew that his selkie wife missed the sea too much to be content on land forever.

So he gave her back her sealskin, as a gift of freedom, and wept salty tears as she swam away from him and their daughter.

But he discovered he couldn't live without his selkie wife. Not even for a day. So he sat at the end of the pier, and she sang to him and he spoke to her. He left their little girl in the care of his brother while he sat, every day, on the seashore with his wife.

After weeks and months of his faithful love, the selkie wife persuaded the sea witches to grant the fisherman the power to join her in the sea, as a seal.

They were both happy together in the sea. But now their little girl was alone on land, with an uncle who hated the seals, hated that they ate his fish and ripped his nets and sang happy songs on the rocks.

And he hated that they'd taken his brother away.

He watched his niece peeling his tatties, cooking his stovies, cleaning his boots, mending his nets, weeding his garden, and as she worked, he saw her look out to sea. He knew that she had selkie blood in her, that she felt the call of the sea, and that she heard the laughter and songs of her parents.

So he told her terrible things about the seal people and the dangers of the sea. But still the girl hummed the seals' music, and gazed at the sea.

So the uncle forbade her to go past their garden gate. He boarded up the window facing the blue-green sea, and let her look only at the brown hills of the land.

Still the girl listened to the waves and the wind, and sang verses of seal song.

So the uncle asked the wise women of the village for advice. He listened to their tales, and he learnt of the one way to keep his niece on land forever.

He learnt that if he cut off all her fingers and all her toes, then she would never be able to swim as a seal. Without fingers or toes, even if she did turn into a seal, her flippers would be too short and stubby for her to swim.

But, he thought, what use is a girl round the house with no fingers? So he decided to cut off only her toes, then she could still mend his nets.

But, he thought, what use is a girl round the garden who can't walk? So he decided to cut off the toes of only one foot, then she could limp around the garden digging up tatties.

But, he thought, what use is a girl in the family who hates me? So he decided to cut off only the tips of her toes, then she wouldn't mind quite so much, and she might still cook his favourite stovies.

He put strong drink and stronger herbs in her cup of tea that night. When she fell asleep, he took off her left sock, picked up his axe, and cut off the top joints of all her left toes. Then he bandaged

her up as she slept, drank the rest of her night-time drink and fell fast asleep himself.

When he woke, she was gone.

Her uncle ran down to the seashore. And among the seals he saw one little seal who was the slowest to scramble up on to the rocks and the last to slip into the sea when he ran towards them. One little seal who then swam and tumbled and flipped in the water just as joyfully and fast as the rest of the young seals.

The uncle wondered if he should have cut off more toes, then perhaps she wouldn't have been able to swim away from him, or if he should have cut off no toes at all, then perhaps she might have stayed with him for longer.

And he listened to one little seal, with one short flipper, singing with her mum and dad in the sea. Singing their happy ending.

Breaking the Spell:
The Story of Tam Linn

This story is about a girl called Janet, but the story starts hundreds of years before Janet was born. It starts with a boy called Tam Linn, who lived a long time ago in the borderlands where Scotland meets England.

One day Tam Linn asked his grandfather, the Earl of Roxburgh, "Am I old enough to go hunting with you and your men?"

"Yes, my boy," said his grandfather. "You can come hunting with me this spring, but only if you promise two things: you must not fall behind, and you must not fall off."

Tam Linn knew why he mustn't fall behind or fall off. It wasn't because of the dangerous animals in the forest – it was because of the fairies.

The fairies in the forest weren't little and twinkly, and they weren't interested in granting wishes. They were as tall as the Earl's soldiers, and they carried swords and spears instead of wands and glitter.

So Tam Linn tried very hard not to fall behind, and not to fall off. But his pony had shorter legs than the men's horses, so Tam Linn did fall behind; his pony was used to galloping on roads and fields,

not on the rough ground of the forest, so his pony stumbled, and he did fall off.

He might have been safe if he'd fallen on moss or mud or thorns. But he fell on a mound of bright green grass. And mounds of bright green grass are often the entrances to the fairies' world.

When Tam Linn landed on his back on the small green hill, the ground opened and hands reached up to drag him down. He was hauled along dark tunnels and thrown at the feet of the Fairy Queen.

Tam Linn looked at the Queen. She was so beautiful that she was terrifying, but he tried not to show his fear. He stood up, he looked straight at the Queen, and he didn't tremble or weep or beg.

Tam Linn was a handsome lad, and the Queen liked the look of him, so she cast a spell on him. A spell which meant that as he grew, he became one of the fairy folk, and that when he reached his full height, he stopped growing old. He became immortal, one of the Fairy Queen's knights forever.

Years passed. And for all of those years the wise elders of the Borders told their young men and young women to avoid Carterhaugh Woods because it was guarded for the Fairy Queen by her fiercest knight.

But one girl, whose name was Janet and whose father was the Laird of Carterhaugh, didn't like being told not to go into her own woods, whoever guarded them.

So one summer day, Janet stepped into the woods, and looked around her. She saw flowers and butterflies, she heard birds singing.

She laughed. These weren't woods to be scared of! They were beautiful!

So she went deeper, until she reached the middle of the woods, where she saw a low stone well and a white horse tied to a tree. "I wonder whose horse that is," Janet said to herself, and she sat down by the well to wait and see.

After a while she noticed a sweet scent coming from a rose bush on the other side of the well. "That rose would look lovely on my dress," she said. Janet leant forward and grasped the stem of the rose, then bent it until it broke.

Suddenly a voice boomed, "Who dares steal the Fairy Queen's flowers?"

A young man stepped out from the trees on the other side of the clearing. He was tall, with long hair, fine clothes and a smooth face. He looked at Janet and said again, in a deep, threatening voice, "Who dares steal the Fairy Queen's flowers?"

Janet stood up straight. "I dare, because I am Janet of Carterhaugh. Who dares question me in my father's wood?"

"I dare, because I am Tam Linn, and I guard this wood for the Fairy Queen. So you will give back that flower."

Janet stared at him, and slowly, carefully, she pinned the rose to the collar of her dress.

Tam Linn could have picked Janet up in one hand and thrown her out of the woods. But he was impressed by the way she stood up to him and looked him in the eye, just as he had tried to do with the Fairy Queen, many years before.

So instead he took Janet by the hand, and offered to show her all the best places in the woods to find and pick flowers.

As they walked through Carterhaugh Woods, they talked.

Janet asked, "Have you always been one of the fairy folk?"

"No," said Tam Linn, "I was once as human as you." He told her how he'd fallen on the green mound, been dragged through the tunnels and flung at the feet of the Fairy Queen.

"Do you *like* being one of the fairy folk?"

Tam Linn sighed. "It's glamorous and powerful and magical, but I have no choices. I must guard this wood forever if the Fairy Queen orders me to."

"Can't you just stop being one of the fairy folk?"

Tam Linn laughed. "It's not that easy. I'd need someone to…"

"To what?"

"To break the Fairy Queen's spell."

"I could do that," said Janet.

"No, you couldn't. It's far too dangerous."

She touched the rose on her collar. "But I'm brave."

"I know you're brave." He smiled. "But I couldn't ask you to do that for me."

"You're not asking me," she said. "I'm offering."

So Tam Linn told her how to break the spell. "Tonight is midsummer's night, when the Fairy Queen parades her army round her lands. At midnight, they will pass through Carterhaugh Woods. If you hide at the well and watch the army go past, you can break the spell.

"The first troop of her soldiers will be led by a knight on a brown horse. Do not let him see you. The second troop will be led by a knight on a black horse. Do not let him hear you. The third troop will be led by a knight on a white horse. That will be me. You will recognise me because I will wear only one glove.

"If you want to break the spell, pull me from my horse and hold me tight. If the Fairy Queen wants to keep me, she will turn me into many loathsome and dangerous beasts. But hold on tight to whatever is in your arms, until I am turned into a flaming torch, and throw that torch into the well. Then the spell will be broken."

Janet promised she would hold on. Then she left the woods and went home, with a big bunch of flowers in her arms.

She waited until night fell. Then she dressed in her darkest dress, put on black boots and a black cloak, and went back to the woods.

She stepped into the trees, and looked around. She heard creaks and rustles, and saw pairs of tiny bright eyes blink out. Now *this* looked like the wood she'd been warned against. But she had made a promise, so she went deeper into the woods until she reached the well. This time she didn't sit by the well, she hid behind it, under the rose bush, and waited until she heard the jingle of harness and the thud of feet.

The Fairy Queen's army paraded past her.

She saw the first troop of soldiers led by a knight on a brown horse, and she crouched down low under the bush so he wouldn't see her.

She saw the second troop of soldiers led by a knight on a black horse, and she held her breath so he wouldn't hear her.

She saw the third troop of soldiers led by a knight on a white horse and she saw that he had one hand gloved and the other bare, so she leapt out from under the bush, grabbed his bare hand, and dragged him from the horse.

His helmet fell off, and she could see Tam Linn's face, pale in the night. So she wrapped her arms round his chest, and she held on tight.

From the back of the army, the Fairy Queen screeched, "LET HIM GO! HE IS MINE!"

But Janet didn't let go.

The Fairy Queen turned Tam Linn into a snake: a great, thick, long, scaly, green serpent. Janet felt the serpent coil round her arms and heard it hiss at her face, but she held on tight.

The Fairy Queen turned Tam Linn into a lion. Janet felt the lion's claws on her shoulders and smelt its hot bloody breath on her face, but she held on tight.

The Fairy Queen turned Tam Linn into a bear. Janet felt the bear's paws squeeze the air from her lungs and felt its thick fur smother her, but she held on tight.

The Fairy Queen turned Tam Linn into a hot bar of iron. Janet smelt her sleeves singe and felt her skin blister, but she held on tight.

The Fairy Queen turned Tam Linn into a bright burning torch. Janet lifted the flaming branch high and threw it into the well. The water hissed and steamed, and Tam Linn stepped out of the well, dripping wet, but smiling.

He took Janet's hand, and the two of them walked out of Carterhaugh Woods, free forever from the Fairy Queen's spells.

Because this is a fairy story, Tam Linn and Janet got married, and they lived happily ever after.

They and their children are long gone now, but the well is still there. So you can visit Tam Linn's Well in Carterhaugh Woods. But don't pick any flowers, because I don't know who guards the woods for the Fairy Queen now…

The Witch of Lochlann

You can't find Lochlann on a map. Not any more. But many years ago, the country of Lochlann was Scotland's main enemy.

Lochlann might have been a kingdom in Scandinavia. It might have been an island in the Atlantic or the North Sea. It might even have been *under* the sea. But wherever Lochlann was found (and it was found in different places at different times) the King of Lochlann was always jealous of Scotland.

He was jealous of Scotland's beautiful mountains, deep glens, fast rivers, fertile farms and abundant fish. But he was most jealous of Scotland's trees. Lochlann was always too wet, cold and windy (wherever it was) for forests of pine, birch, oak, hazel and rowan to grow. So the King of Lochlann decided that if he couldn't have lovely trees, neither should his enemy Scotland.

He asked his stepmother, who was a powerful witch, to burn down the trees of Scotland.

The Witch of Lochlann summoned her silver chariot, pulled by her red dogs. But her chariot was shiny and her dogs were huge, and she didn't want to be seen as she flew over Scotland. So she harnessed a big black rain cloud, and tied it with magic under the chariot's axle and the dogs' bellies, to hide them as they flew.

She flew through the sky to Scotland, and she threw fireballs onto the forests of Ettrick, then Galloway. The Witch of Lochlann couldn't see the trees burn, because the black cloud hid the land from her, but she could smell the sap boiling and hear the snap and crack of trees falling.

However, the people of Scotland could see the forests burning. They saw the black cloud above and the grey smoke below, and the fireballs being flung down between. They saw flames creep close to their homes; they saw wolves and bears run out of the burning forest towards them.

The King of Scotland ordered his warriors to stop the Witch of Lochlann burning any more trees. So the next day his greatest warriors stood on hilltops and tall towers. They tried to attack her as she flew overhead, throwing down fire on Argyll, then the Trossachs. But they couldn't see her through the thick black cloud.

So the next day, as she was burning the trees of Birnam, then Deeside, the warriors bowed before the King and said, "We can't fight what we can't see!"

Then a tall weather-beaten man stepped out of the wailing crowd of homeless and scared people. He said, "Warriors can't fight what they can't see. But I am a hunter, and I often hunt what I can't see. Let me hunt the witch. Let me track her. Let me lure her out. And let me stop her."

So, carrying a letter ordering the King's subjects to help him as he hunted the Witch of Lochlann, the hunter climbed to the top of the tallest mountain. He saw the trail of smoke and ash sweep across the wide southern lands of Scotland, and the trail of embers

and smouldering trees curve up the middle of Scotland. The hunter worked out that the next day, the Witch of Lochlann would be aiming her fireballs at Moray.

He ran down the mountain, rode the King's fastest horse to Moray, and showed the local farmers the King's letter.

Just before dawn, the farmers took all the mother animals from their farms, and put them on one bank of the wide river Spey. Then they took all the baby animals, and put them on the other bank.

So the horses, cows, sheep, pigs and goats were on one side of the Spey. And the foals, calves, lambs, piglets and kids were on the other side of the Spey.

They missed each other.

And they called to each other.

As the sun came up and the black cloud flew in from Lochlann, the horses and foals neighed at each other, the cows and calves mooed at each other, the sheep and lambs baaed at each other, the pigs and piglets snorted at each other, and the goats and kids bleated at each other.

The noise was incredible. Loud. And sad.

The Witch of Lochlann flew over Moray, throwing down fireballs, and she heard the noise. The loudness and the sadness.

She wondered what it was.

She looked down, but she couldn't see past the black cloud. She peered over the side of her chariot, but she still couldn't see.

So she leant over further, to see what was making the noise. Her head appeared over the side of the black cloud and the hunter, who was standing on a hill with his bow ready, shot the witch through the eye.

She fell back, dead, into her chariot, which was pulled by her red dogs back to Lochlann, wherever Lochlann was that year.

As the witch's magic died, the cloud was released from her spell. It was torn from the axle of the chariot and the bellies of the dogs, and it ripped open.

So it rained. The cloud threw down, not fire, but water. The fires went out, all over Scotland. The trees of Moray and the trees of Scotland were safe again.

The baby animals were brought back over the river Spey, and once they were with their mothers again, they were happy and quiet. So the people of Scotland had peace to celebrate the death of the Witch of Lochlann, and the skill of the hunter who had lured out his prey.

The Loch Fada Kelpie

My mum grew up on the Isle of Skye. At the weekends, her dad took her with him when he went up to Loch Fada to fish and to watch birds.

But he didn't catch many fish or see many birds with a noisy little girl running about the water's edge. So, as he polished his binoculars and chose the right fishing flies out of his box, he used to tell my mum to go off and play. Near a deep loch and high cliffs! But he was a sensible man, and he always gave my mum a whistle. "Just in case," he said. I assumed, until recently, that the 'just in case' was in case she fell in the water or got stuck on the cliff or sprained her ankle.

But now, since my last visit to Skye, I've started to wonder if the whistle was for another 'just in case' entirely.

Because Loch Fada has a kelpie.

A kelpie is hard to describe, because most of the time it's under the water, and very few people have seen its underwater shape and lived. But when it comes out of the loch, a kelpie takes the form of a horse with a splendid saddle and bridle, and waits by the lochside for a young man or a young woman to climb up for a ride.

Then the kelpie gallops towards the water, and the rider is stuck to the saddle and can't get off, so the rider is pulled deep down under.

No one who rides a kelpie is ever seen again, though sometimes their lungs, still filled with their panicked last breath, float up to the surface.

And we know that Loch Fada has a kelpie, because many years before my mum played there, a little girl called Isobel often went to the loch with her dad, when he went fishing and peat-cutting.

Just like my grandad, he didn't want a noisy little girl disturbing the fish. So as he laid his peat iron – his *tairsgeir* – down at the peat bank, then went to the lochside and got his bait out of his bag, he always told Isobel to go off and play.

Isobel loved that, because she dreamt of being an explorer when she grew up. So by the lochside, under the Old Man of Storr and on the edge of the sea cliffs, Isobel would explore the Amazon, the Sahara and the Karakorum Pass.

Then one day she saw the very thing that every explorer needs: a beautiful white horse, by the edge of the loch.

Isobel looked round, but there was no one nearby. She thought it wouldn't do any harm to chat to the horse. So she approached carefully to make friends with it, speaking calmly and untangling its long white mane.

She was surprised that the horse's mane was damp, though it hadn't rained on Skye since the day before, and even more surprised to discover that the tangles were caused by lumps of waterweed. Then she glanced down at the white horse's hooves. It had no horseshoes.

Isobel patted its mane and leant closer to the horse's neck, to look at its bridle. The bridle was made of soft leather with delicate stitching, but no metal.

Isobel suddenly knew that she was standing beside a kelpie.

A kelpie with waterweed in its mane because it had risen out of the loch.

A kelpie with no iron near its body because magical beings can't stand cold iron.

A kelpie which planned to drown her and eat her.

So Isobel stepped away, and the beautiful white horse stepped after her. She backed further off and the kelpie followed.

She turned and ran. The horse trotted after her. She felt its breath on her neck, she screamed and ran faster, but the kelpie kept pace.

Isobel was running as fast as she could on her two short legs, but the horse was chasing her on its four long strong legs. She was going as fast as she could, and it was barely breaking into a canter.

Soon the horse was at her shoulder, running beside her. Nudging her, pushing her, herding her towards the edge of the loch.

So instead of trying to outrun the horse, Isobel slowed her pace. She ducked down, she dived under the horse's belly, and she rolled on the heather towards her dad's peat-bank.

The kelpie, at last worried that she might get away, finally broke into a gallop. Isobel held up the tairsgeir, and the kelpie galloped right on to the shining metal blade. The iron split the kelpie's fine white skin, and roasted its wet red flesh. The kelpie screamed and limped back to the loch.

Isobel stood up and watched as it vanished under the water, and she saw, as no other living person had seen, what shape the kelpie took under the clear water of the loch.

That shape was too horrible to describe to anyone else, but she did tell everyone that there was a kelpie in Loch Fada. And local families have been careful there ever since.

So I wonder if the kelpie was the 'just in case' which my grandfather was protecting my mum against. Because the whistle he gave her was made of iron. And because in all her days playing by the loch, she never saw a kelpie.

But I wonder if the kelpie saw her.

Whuppity Stoorie

A long time ago, the most dangerous place in Scotland wasn't the border or the mountains or the cliffs. The most dangerous place in Scotland was the edge of the forest.

The forest was filled with magical beings who weren't always kind to people. Sometimes they played tricks, sometimes they were cruel, and sometimes they stole children.

So, if you lived near the forest, you had to be very careful not to say or do anything which might attract the attention of the beings who lived there.

Long ago a young woman called Kate had a farm at the edge of the forest. All she had on that farm were a couple of stony fields, her wee son Jamie, and a big pink pig.

That big pink pig was their hope for the future, because the pig was due to have piglets. If the piglets were healthy and plump, then Kate could sell them to buy food for the winter and seeds to plant in the spring. So Kate and Jamie fed the pig better than they fed themselves.

One day, Kate sent Jamie off to the pig's sty with a big bowl of turnips and oats. But then she heard him yell, "Mum! Come here!"

Kate ran into the sty and found the pig lying on the floor. The pig wasn't pink any more, she was grey, and she was struggling to breathe. Her ribs were creaking and rattling with every slow breath.

Kate had worked on farms her whole life, and she knew the pig had to get back up on her feet if she was to have a chance. So Kate and Jamie put their hands under the pig and tried to lift her up. But they had fed the pig too well, and she was too heavy.

So they tried to persuade the pig to get up herself. They put mustard on her trotters, but she didn't get up. They put a clothes peg on her tail, but she didn't get up. They even put pepper under her nose – *aaaa choo* – but she didn't get up.

Finally, as the pig got greyer and her breathing got slower, Kate said to Jamie, "Bring me the red tartan blanket to keep the pig warm, then off you go to bed. I'll stay up and keep her company, because I don't think she'll still be with us in the morning."

Kate sat there, shivering, as she thought of the hungry winter and bare fields she and Jamie would have without any piglets to sell.

She heard the pig groaning, so she reached out and patted the pig's flank. She sniffed back tears, and said, "I'd give anything, *anything*, to have my pig well again."

As soon as she said 'I'd give anything' there was a bright light at the edge of the forest, a light which whirled and birled all the way to the door of the pigsty.

"You'd give *anything*?" said a voice at the door.

Kate turned round, and saw a wee old wifie dressed all in green: green boots, green cloak, green dress, green apron, green pointy hat.

The wee old wifie reached into the pocket of her apron and pulled out a wee green bottle.

She stepped into the sty and repeated, "You'd give anything!" She tipped the bottle up, and poured one bright green drop on to the pig's snout, one drop between the pig's ears and one drop on the pig's tail.

The pig snorted, leapt to her feet, and stuck her snout in the bowl of porridge.

Kate was so happy that she didn't even notice the wee old wifie whirling back to the forest. In fact Kate was so busy that night helping the big pink pig give birth to a litter of twelve plump piglets that she completely forgot about the wee old wifie.

But the next evening Kate heard a knock at the door, and there on the doorstep was the wee old wifie dressed all in green.

"Oh, hello!" said Kate. "Thank you so much for healing my pig."

"I've come for what you promised me," said the wee old wifie.

"I didn't promise you anything, did I? But you did heal my pig, so I should give you something to say thank you."

Kate offered the wee old wifie the red blanket. "It smells a bit of pig but it's very warm."

"It is not a blanket you owe me."

"What about my granny's old milkjug? It's a bit chipped, but it has pretty blue flowers on it."

"It is not a jug you owe me."

"I've not got anything else… oh! What about a piglet? That would be fitting. When they're weaned, I shall give you a piglet."

"It is not a piglet you owe me. I'm here for your son, Jamie."

"Jamie? My son? But you can't take my son! You can't take someone's child!"

"You said you'd give *anything* and he's the only thing I want."

"But you can't! There must be rules…"

The old wifie nodded reluctantly. "The rules I live by say I can't take him until three nights after the promise and I can't take him at all if you call me by my true name."

"So if I call you by your true name, you can't take my son?"

The old wifie nodded, then laughed. "Aye, but you'll never guess it." And she whirled off to the edge of the forest.

Kate sat by the fire, wrapped in the blanket, and she thought and thought. What could the old wifie's name be? She was a strange wee woman, so maybe she had a strange name.

Whirligig?

Greenboots?

Nebby Nora?

But none of those seemed right, so Kate thought of all the names she'd ever heard. Her head filled with the names of her friends, her family, her neighbours and the people in stories her granny had told her (*Janet, Flora, Isobel, Helen, Sheherazade, Utha* and *Skiach*) until her head was almost full.

Kate sat and thought of names all night, all day and all the next night, until she had a horrible headache. So she went out into the fresh air to see if that would help clear all the wrong names out of her head and leave just one.

She went for a walk along the edge of the forest (which wasn't so dangerous by daylight, and anyway Kate was a brave woman). But walking in the forest was no help because she kept seeing flowers which reminded her of more names.

"She could be called *Daisy* or *Lily* or *Lavender* or *Ivy* or *Nettle* or *Thistle*, or even *Rosebaywillowherb*. She could be called *anything*!"

Kate's head was full to bursting. She slumped down on a tree stump and put her head in her hands.

Then she heard a laugh, coming from under the tree stump. She bent down and saw a wee hole, and through the wee hole she saw a wee house, and in the wee house she saw a wee wifie. A wee old wifie dressed all in green.

The wee old wifie was spinning, and as she spun, she chanted to herself:

> "*Little kens the guid wife at hame,*
> *That Whuppity Stoorie is ma name.*
> *What she doesna ken, she canna say,*
> *And the bairn will be mine the morra's day.*"

She laughed, and repeated the rhyme again and again as she spun.

Up on the tree stump, Kate laughed too. Very quietly. Because now her head was clear. All the other names had vanished and one name shone bright in front of her eyes.

She was so happy, she ran home and hugged Jamie. She was so happy, she hugged the piglets too!

She sat down and waited for night to fall.

There was a knock at the door. "I've come for what you promised me. I've come for your son Jamie."

"Oh no! First I get to guess your name. How many guesses do I get?"

"Three is a good number. You can have three guesses."

"Is your name … *Sheherazade*?"

"Do I look like a *Sheherazade*?"

"No, you certainly don't. So is your name *Rosebaywillowherb*?"

"Do I look like a *Rosebaywillowherb*?"

"No, you certainly don't. You look like a … *Whuppity Stoorie!*"

As soon as Kate said her true name, the wee old wifie dressed all in green squealed, and started to turn on the spot. Whuppity Stoorie whirled so fast that she whirled right up into the sky. And she rose so high that she was never seen again.

Because once we know the true names of the magical ones in the forest they have no power over us!

But unless you know ALL their names you should never say 'I'd give anything' in the middle of the night, on the edge of the forest. Not unless you really mean it….

The Ring of Brodgar

In the Orkney islands, there's a ring of stones between two lochs. Dozens of grey stones stand tall in a circle on a hill. And one other lonely stone stands all on its own a few steps away.

Historians and archaeologists will tell you how Neolithic people quarried stones, dug holes, and built this circle millennia ago, and how it took them many long years. It's a great tale of human strength, ingenuity and initiative.

But the locals tell another tale about the Ring of Brodgar. Their tale isn't about people. It's about giants.

Long before people lived in Orkney, even earlier than Once Upon A Time, the seventy islands of Orkney were home to giants. Giants who only came out at night. Each giant lived on a different island, because they were clumsy and often trod on each other's toes in the dark if they lived too close together.

But they were friendly giants, to other giants anyway, and they waved at each other in the moonlight, and sometimes they shouted across the narrow water to arrange parties with each other.

One year, they arranged a midsummer night's party on the mainland of Orkney.

They all brought food: roast deer haunches which they ate like chicken drumsticks, bannocks the size of tables, honeycakes the size of sofas and jugs of heather ale the size of baths.

They sang songs, asked riddles, and told stories.

Then the giant from Hoy took out a fiddle as big as a cow, and a bow as long as a birch tree is high, and he started to play.

The other giants got up to dance. They jumped and they twirled.

And let me tell you, dozens of giants dancing is nothing like a ballet class. No tutus, no pointy toes, no delicate arms raised like wings. A giants' dance is stomping and thumping, crashing and banging, yelling and treading on each other's toes. The only way the giants could avoid stepping on each other was to dance in a circle, following each other, but keeping a safe distance from each other's toes.

As they spun and jumped and thumped, the fiddling giant stepped to the side to keep his own toes and fiddle safe. He played fast and slow, high and low.

The giants clapped and cheered and asked for just one more dance. They were having so much fun that they forgot it was midsummer's night, they forgot that midsummer's night is the shortest night of the year and they forgot why giants only come out at night…

As the giants danced, the sun came up, the sunlight hit the giants and every single one of them turned to STONE.

Dozens of stones in a circle. One stone on its own.

And that's how the Ring of Brodgar was really built. In one very short night!

The King of the Black Art

Once there was a boy whose mother and father were too poor to set him up in a job. They had no money to buy him a boat, so he couldn't become a fisherman. They had no money to buy him a sword, so he couldn't become a soldier. They had no money to buy him a cart, so he couldn't become a merchant. They didn't even have enough money to apprentice him to a builder, cobbler or joiner, for him to learn a trade. They were worried their boy would never have a proper job.

Then, one day, a man rode past their little house. A man on a tall black horse, with a billowing black cloak and a jutting black beard. He saw the boy digging in the garden, and his dark eyes opened wide.

He shouted for the boy's parents, and from high on his horse he called, "I wish to take your boy as my apprentice. He looks like he has a talent for my line of work."

"But sir, we don't have money to pay for an apprenticeship."

"Then I'll take him as my apprentice for free, so long as you let me have him for a year and a day."

"Thank you, sir! Will you bring him back to us after a year and a day?"

"No, you'll have to come and fetch him, and you will only get him back if you can still recognise him."

The boy's parents looked at their son. They'd known him all his life, so even if he got a bit taller, a bit wider, a bit more untidy without his mum to trim his hair, they were sure they'd still recognise him.

So his father said, "Yes, you can have him as your apprentice for a year and a day, and I'll fetch him at the end of it."

The man in black leant down, and pulled the boy up on to the back of his saddle. Then the big black horse reared up and galloped off.

Just before the horse turned the corner, the boy's father yelled after them, "Where do I come in a year and a day?"

The man's voice echoed round the glen. "Just ask for the castle of the King of the Black Art."

But neither of the boy's parents thought to ask, not until it was too late, what the man's trade was, and what their son would be learning...

∾ ☯ ∾

When the year and a day were up, it was time for the father to bring his son home. He followed the same path as the horse and asked everyone he met if they knew the way to the castle of the King of the Black Art. He was directed towards mountains, over rivers, through forests and into the deep heart of Scotland.

Then he saw it. A castle so tall, so wide, so solid, that it was like walking up to a cliff.

He banged on the door, the door swung open, and he walked up a long echoing corridor until he came to a courtyard,

where the King of the Black Art stood, his huge cloak wrapped round his body.

"You've come for your son?" The King of the Black Art laughed. "He's the best apprentice I've ever had, and I don't want to give him back. So you can't have him unless you can recognise him."

The king flung open his cloak and twenty-one pigeons flew out. The birds started to circle the courtyard. All the pigeons looked exactly the same, all plump and healthy, with feathers shining green and purple.

The father had no idea how to recognise his son, until he noticed that twenty pigeons were flying anticlockwise round the courtyard and only one pigeon was flying clockwise. So he pointed to it. "That's my son!"

The King of the Black Art scowled, the pigeon fell out of the air and the boy bumped on to the flagstones of the courtyard.

The boy leapt up, grabbed his father's hand and yelled, "RUN!"

They ran out of the courtyard, through the corridor, out of the door and away from the castle as fast as they could. As they ran, the boy whispered, "The King of the Black Art is a magician, and he's taught me so much!"

"I've not taught you enough," a voice boomed behind them. "I've not finished with you yet. I'll have you back within the day!"

The boy laughed and kept on running. When at last they were out of sight and sound of the castle, he let his father slow to a walk. "He didn't pay me a thing," the boy said. "All that work for him, and I haven't earned a single penny."

"You were an apprentice," gasped his father. "We didn't expect you to come home with jingly pockets."

"But wouldn't it be nice to take some money home to Mother? We can use my magic to get a bit of gold."

"How?"

The boy smiled. "You have to sell me."

"Sell you? I don't want to sell you. I've only just got you back!"

"You don't have to sell me for long. I'll turn myself into a dog, and you can sell the dog at the next village. But if you make sure you keep the dog's collar, then by the time you're out of the village, I'll be walking beside you again."

Suddenly, the boy was gone, and there on the path was a beautiful dog, a hunting hound with long legs, a sharp clever face, and a wide leather collar.

His father took the dog to the village square and when people thought of all the deer this long-legged hound could catch, they offered lots of money to buy it. One woman offered a whole purse of coins.

The father took the purse and gave her the dog, but he kept the collar. "For sentimental reasons," he said.

He held tight to the collar as he walked out of the village, and suddenly there was his son beside him, laughing and saying, "Next time, let's sell something bigger, and we'll get even more gold."

As they approached a town, the boy said, "I'll change into a horse, and you can sell me again. But remember, don't sell the bridle and reins. Keep them tight in your hand, and I'll be beside you before you're out of the town."

And there on the grass stood a huge chestnut stallion, with a bright red bridle and reins, looking fast enough to win races, and strong enough to carry a knight in armour. When the father led the horse into the marketplace, people thronged round, keen to buy this splendid horse. They offered bags of gold.

A man at the back, in a dark hooded cloak, offered a whole *pile* of gold.

The father said, "Sold! Sold to the man with the pile of gold."

"Ah, but I want to try before I buy," said the hooded man. "I want to ride the horse, to see if he is as fast and strong as he looks."

The father frowned.

"I'll leave all this gold as a deposit," said the man, "as a promise that I will turn the horse round before I reach the edge of the town."

The father looked at the gold, and thought, 'It is fair to try before you buy.' So he helped the man on to the horse's back and threw up the red reins.

He stood by the pile of gold and watched the horse and rider gallop along the street. But when they reached the edge of the town the man didn't turn round, he forced the horse to gallop out of town. And the wind blew the man's hood back, so the father could see the jutting beard of the King of the Black Art.

At the father's feet, the pile of gold had turned into a pile of steaming horse dung....

By the time the King of the Black Art had ridden all the way back to the castle, the horse was dripping with sweat. The King of the Black Art said to his groom, "Brush him down, feed him, and give him water, but whatever you do, don't take that bridle off. I don't want him getting away again, not until I've used up all of his talent."

The groom brushed the horse down, fed the horse hay, and then took him to the river to drink. But the horse couldn't seem to get his head all the way down to the water, and the groom wondered if that bridle was too tight. It wouldn't do any harm to loosen it a little bit…

As soon as he undid the buckle, the horse turned into a salmon, which leapt into the river. The long silver salmon started to swim as fast as it could down the river, away from the castle.

But the King of the Black Art heard the groom shouting and jumped out of the window of his tower, turning into an otter as he fell.

The smooth strong otter splashed into the river, and swam after the salmon, sharp white teeth snapping and biting at the salmon's flashing silver tail.

The salmon leapt out of the river, and as water drops flew from the fish's fins, it changed into a swallow.

The fast bird flew through the breeze away from the castle, but the otter clambered out of the river and turned into a hawk.

The hawk flew up and up and up until it was high above the swallow, then it started to dive. And a hawk diving is the fastest thing

on earth! The hawk dived straight down at the swallow, its hooked beak and ripping talons ready to grasp and tear.

The swallow turned into a grain of barley, and fell into the corner of a farmyard. The hawk swooped down, and turned into a cockerel. The cockerel started to peck, to pick up and gulp down every grain of barley in that farmyard, until the cockerel was so fat and full it couldn't even move its legs.

Then the last grain of barley left in the farmyard, the grain of barley right in the corner, turned into a fox. The fox walked up to the cockerel and *bit its head off!*

That was the end of the King of the Black Art.

But it was only the beginning for his apprentice!

The Monster of Raasay

Once there was a crofter who lived on his own, because he'd been rude to his wife, cruel to his sons and ignored his daughters. He was sad and lonely, but he was sure he'd be happy if only he had a bigger house.

One day, he was walking round his croft on the isle of Raasay when he heard a squeak. He looked down and saw a fluffy little creature.

It had long black fur, big silver eyes, tiny white teeth and little pink paws. It squeaked at him.

He picked the creature up, took it home, put it on his table and poked at it. He poked at it until it cried.

When it cried, there was a roar outside his window. "Leave my baby alone!"

The crofter looked out of the window and saw a monster. She had shaggy black hair, huge silver eyes, long white fangs and curved pink claws. She was a bigger, less squeaky version of the animal on the table.

But the monster was far too big to get in through the window, and the door was locked. So the crofter smiled.

"Give me back my baby!" roared the monster.

The baby squealed, "Muummmy!"

The crofter put his hand over the baby's mouth and said, "I'll only give you back your baby if you do three tasks for me. First, clear my fields of pebbles and rocks so I can plough more easily."

The monster, who lived in the earth and had power over the stones, cleared the fields easily. She stomped back to the window. "Give me back my baby!"

"Not yet. Now I want you to build me a new house, a house three times as big as this one, with two doors so I don't have to share with the animals."

The monster had power over the earth and the stones and the trees, so she built the house easily. "NOW give me back my baby!"

"Not yet. For your last task, I want you to thatch the roof of my new house with feathers of all different colours, from a hundred different birds."

The mother monster wailed. She didn't have power over the air or the birds, so she would never be able to gather enough feathers to thatch a whole roof, and she would never get her baby back.

She wailed and roared and howled. The baby squeaked and cried and sobbed.

The crofter laughed. He didn't really need a feathery roof, but he thought a monster who would work for him every day until he gave her baby back would be quite useful.

But as she wept and the baby sobbed and the crofter laughed, the noise reached the mainland. And all the mother birds who had ever sat on a nest and felt an egg crack open and fed a baby bird's

wide-open mouth, heard this mother monster wail for her baby and they flew over to Raasay.

Every single mother bird plucked one feather from her tail and let it fall down on to the roof of the new crofthouse.

Soon the roof was thatched with feathers of every possible colour. The crofter grunted, and handed the monster her shivering little baby.

The mother monster and her baby went back to their dark muddy hole in the ground, and cuddled, and wiped each other's eyes. The crofter moved into his big fancy feathered house, all on his own.

Who do you think was happier?

School for Heroes

Many centuries ago, there was a school high in the jagged black mountains of Skye. It was a school for heroes, run by the warrior Skiach and her daughter Utha.

They taught sword-fighting, wrestling, gorge-leaping and the hero's call. Most hero schools taught those subjects, but Skiach's school for heroes was famous because she had invented a new weapon, the Gae Bolg.

This was a long heavy spear, with extra barbs behind the blade, barbs which curved backwards, so that when you jabbed it into an enemy's belly, it was very hard for them to pull it out. In fact, the only way to get your enemy off the Gae Bolg was to wait until they were dead, then put your foot on their belly and tug the spearhead out. Or else you could cut their flesh away to free the blade.

The Gae Bolg was a battle-winning weapon, because very few warriors were brave enough to face it. But it wasn't easy to use. The extra barbs made it heavy and unwieldy, so it needed careful handling. The only warrior who could teach you how to use it was Skiach herself.

That's why warriors and heroes came to her school in the black mountains of Skye.

One autumn, an Irish warrior called Cuchullin decided to learn the Gae Bolg. He was already a great hero, so fierce in a fight that afterwards he had to be dipped in three barrels of water to take the heat of battle out of him. The first barrel boiled away, the second simmered, and the third was still hot enough to scald.

So Cuchullin crossed over the sea to Skye in seven steps, to ask Skiach to teach him.

He strode up the mountain, and knocked on the door. Skiach and Utha opened the door, and found this big hairy hero standing proud on their doorstep. "I am here! I have arrived! I have come to make you and your school famous! It is I, Cuchullin, the great hero!"

Skiach and Utha looked at him, then looked at each other.

Skiach turned back to Cuchullin. "If you're already a great hero, then you don't need to learn anything from me." She slammed the door in his face.

But Cuchullin wasn't a man to let doors slam in his face. So he thumped and battered at the door until the school shook, until the mountains of Skye shook.

Skiach said to Utha, "Daughter, go and get rid of that arrogant young man."

So Utha went out to get rid of Cuchullin. He wasn't a man to let doors slam in his face, and he wasn't an easy man to get rid of either, so eventually Utha had to challenge him to a fight.

Utha was a skilled warrior who had learnt all the lessons her mother's school for heroes had to teach, so it was a fearsome battle. They fought with daggers, with spears, with bows and arrows, with chariots, with swords and shields.

They fought for a day and a night and a day. They fought over all the mountains of Skye, the sharp black mountains and the round red mountains.

They matched each other stroke for stroke, until Cuchullin saw his chance. When Utha had her sword high in the air, Cuchullin threw away his sword, grabbed the rim of Utha's shield with both hands and *twisted* it round, breaking the fingers behind it.

Utha couldn't fight with a broken hand, so she had to admit defeat.

Skiach was so angry at what Cuchullin had done to her daughter that she grabbed her Gae Bolg from behind the door, and rushed out to challenge him herself. To punish and kill him.

Cuchullin had come to Skye to learn the Gae Bolg, but he hadn't expected his first lesson to be defending himself against it!

In her first attack, Skiach drove the vicious barbed spear towards his throat, his chest, his belly, his thigh. But Cuchullin parried, he evaded, he avoided, he leapt out of the way. As Skiach attacked again and again, he invented ways of defending himself against the Gae Bolg that no other hero had ever discovered.

They fought all round the black and red mountains, and the mountains trembled under their feet. They were so evenly matched that they fought in the mountains for seven days and seven nights.

Utha, whose hand was now bound up, watched and worried. Her mother had never before taken so long to win. Utha worried that her mother might *not* win. She worried that her mother might be beaten, that she might be injured, or even killed.

She worried about the reputation of their school for heroes.

She decided that she had to stop the fight.

So she kneaded a loaf of bread, one-handed, then lit a fire and began to bake the loaf. Soon the smell of fresh bread wafted round the mountains.

Utha called, "Mother! Cuchullin! Stop for just long enough to break bread together."

The smell of fresh bread was tempting, but the heat of battle was too strong in their blood and they couldn't stop fighting.

So Utha hunted along the slopes of the mountains, shot a deer, and roasted the deer on the fire. The smell of roasting venison wafted around the mountains.

Utha called, "Mother! Cuchullin! Take a break just long enough to eat meat together."

The smell of the venison was mouthwatering, but the heat of battle was too strong in their blood and they couldn't stop fighting.

So Utha searched along the foot of the mountains until she found a hazel tree. She counted its hazel nuts. There were only nine nuts growing on the whole tree, so she knew that these must be the hazelnuts of wisdom, hazelnuts which would bring wisdom to any who tasted them.

So she picked the nuts, laid them over the embers of the fire, and the smell of toasting nuts wafted round the mountains.

Utha called, "Mother! Cuchullin! Take a break for just long enough to eat these hazelnuts."

Skiach and Cuchullin smelt the toasting nuts. They both recognised the hazelnuts of wisdom, and they both wondered if the nuts would give them all the knowledge in the world. Because someone with all the knowledge in the world would know exactly how to defeat their opponent.

They both threw down their weapons, raced each other to the fire, and reached Utha at exactly the same time.

Skiach and Cuchullin grabbed a hazelnut each and touched it to their lips at exactly the same moment.

But they didn't get the knowledge to defeat their opponent. Instead they both got the wisdom to know that they never could.

They were both wise enough to know that they were evenly matched, that they could fight in the mountains until the end of their energy, the end of their days, the end of time, and that neither of them would ever win.

They were wise enough to shake hands and call it a draw.

So Cuchullin stayed at the school for heroes for a year and a day, and learnt to attack with the Gae Bolg as well as defend against it.

And in honour of the greatest warrior she had ever fought, the greatest warrior she had ever taught or learnt from, Skiach named the black and red mountains of Skye after Cuchullin.

Skiach named the mountains the Cuillins, in memory of the days and nights of those two epic fights.

The Three Questions

Once there was a small school in a small town at the bottom of a small hill which had a small castle at the top.

The teacher in the small school was quite small too, but he had a big voice.

A big, loud, shouty voice.

He used his loud voice all the time. He shouted at all his pupils.

He shouted at them for spelling *eenuff, fisiks* and *rong,* wrong.

He shouted at them for dropping pencils, for sneezing and hiccupping, and for not knowing things he hadn't told them yet.

He shouted at new pupils on their first day of school, and he made them cry. Then he shouted at them for crying.

He shouted at his staff too, even though he didn't have a very big staff – just one former pupil, a girl who cleaned the blackboard, emptied the bins, washed the windows, and swept the ashes out of the fireplace.

One day, the queen who lived in the small castle on the hill was riding past the school. She heard the teacher yelling at the class, and heard a new girl start to cry.

So she summoned the teacher outside.

The teacher thought, "Ooooh, the queen!" and put on his long fur-lined cloak and his big broad-brimmed hat before he went out to meet her.

"Why were you shouting at the children?" asked the queen.

"Well, Ma'am, your majesty." He bowed. "It's the only way they will learn, Ma'am. It makes them scared, you see, and fear is a great teacher, Ma'am, your majesty, Ma'am."

"I'm sure there are better ways to teach people than by fear," said the queen, "but if you think fear is the best way, let's see how it works on you. Come up to my castle tomorrow morning to answer three questions. If you get them wrong, then you'll lose your job as this town's teacher. In fact, if you get them wrong, you'll lose your head."

When he got back to his desk, the teacher was shaking under his hat and inside his cloak. Because the teacher was great at shouting questions like:

"What's 7 x 3?"

"Who sniggered?"

"What's the capital of Lochlann?"

"Who made that puddle?"

And he was great at shouting at his pupils if they didn't get the answers right.

But he was useless at answering questions.

So when he got up the next morning, he called the girl who swept the ashes, he gave her the fur-lined cloak and the broad-brimmed hat, and he whispered to her, "*You* will go up to the castle, *you* will answer those three questions, and *you* will lose your head if you don't get them right."

So the girl walked up to the castle. She hid her face in the shadow of the broad-brimmed hat, and she knocked on the door.

The queen let her in, and said, "Right, teacher. Here is the first question. *If you feed me, I grow; but if you give me a drink, I die. What am I?*"

The girl, who swept the ashes every day, smiled under the hat and said, "A fire."

"Well done," said the queen. "Perhaps you're brighter than I thought. Here is the second question. *When will you find a cherry without a stone?*"

The girl under the hat thought for a moment, then she smiled again and answered, "In the spring, when the cherry tree is in blossom, then the flowers are cherries without stones."

The queen frowned. "I'll have to ask you a very hard third question, the hardest question possible. *What am I thinking right now?*"

The girl grinned. "You're thinking I'm that grumpy old teacher." She pushed the hat back to show her face. "But I'm just the girl who sweeps the ashes!"

The queen laughed. "No, you're not! You answered all the questions so well, now *you* are the teacher, and that grumpy old man can sweep out the fire and clean the blackboard for you."

That's why, nowadays, all teachers are clever and kind and very good at riddles, and none of them ever shout. Do they?

Note from the Author

All of these Scottish tales are stories I tell regularly in schools and libraries (and castles and tents and gardens and caves…) all round Scotland. As with any story told often, they've changed as I tell them. What I've written is very much what I tell, so the stories are not exactly as I first heard or read them, they're the versions that have grown in my head, the versions that have come to life as I tell them to real audiences. So these are my stories, and I hope they will become your stories too, because stories are only really alive when they are shared and passed on.

The Selkie's Toes

There are many wonderful selkie stories from all over Scotland, but this one moves me most because it is about the effect on a child of having a selkie background. I found it in Duncan Williamson's *Tales of the Seal People*, and adapted it as I told it.

Breaking the Spell: The Story of Tam Linn

I believe this is the greatest Scottish fairy tale, with romance and action and a real heroine. There are many versions of Tam Linn. The story I tell is influenced most by the first version I read many years ago in *The Silver Chanter* by Wendy Wood, but also by the song in *Border Ballads* edited by Graham R Tomson.

The Witch of Lochlann

I first found a version of this Speyside story in *Scottish Wonder Tales from Myth and Legend* by Alexander McKenzie, and I really like the difference between the way the warriors work and the way the hunter works.

The Loch Fada Kelpie

Most kelpie stories are similar: stern and scary warnings not to go near the water's edge. There really is a legend about a kelpie in Loch Fada, which is north of Portree on the Isle of Skye. My grandfather really did give my mum a whistle when she played there. How much else is true? You decide!

Whuppity Stoorie

No, it's not a Scottish version of Rumpelstiltskin! No more than Rumpelstiltskin is a German version of Whuppity Stoorie. They are similar tales, and probably share a common great great granny long ago, but they are also quite different. I like that the cause of the silly promise here is a sick pig, not a desire to impress a king! The version I tell is inspired by Wendy Wood's *Silver Chanter* collection.

The Ring of Brodgar

The Ring of Brodgar is a windswept, beautiful place. Not all the original stones are still standing, but the two dozen or so which are left are very impressive, and the one stone on its own does look lonely. I first found this tale in *The Mermaid Bride and Other Orkney Folk Tales* by Tom Muir, and I tell it to infants as often as I can. (I wrote it up for this book outside my daughter's ballet class, and the little girls in leotards sounded very much like giants thumping about!)

The King of the Black Art

This is a story which was kept alive by the travelling people of Perthshire. It's my favourite chase story, so I tell it regularly and I've probably changed it a fair bit, but I first found it in *The King o' the Black Art and Other Folk Tales* by Sheila Douglas, and it's also in Katherine Briggs' *British Folk Tales and Legends, A Sampler.*

The Monster of Raasay

I first found this story in Otta Swire's *Skye, the Island and its Legends*. (Raasay is a long thin island to the east of Skye.) I love the strength of the mother monster's love. It makes me smile and almost cry at the same time. I tell it to kids, but always watch the mums at the back!

School For Heroes

Irish heroes starred in lots of old Scottish legends, because a long time ago the sea linked lands, rather than separated them, so Ireland and Scotland were very close. There are many versions of this legend told from the Irish point of view, but I first found this one in *Skye, the Island and its Legends* by Otta Swire.

The Three Questions

This is a story that turns up in many cultures and with many different riddles, though the last one is always 'What am I thinking?' I adapted this version from a story told in Mull about priests, which I found in *Scottish Traditional Tales* by AL Bruford and DA MacDonald. I love riddles, and sometimes change the first two riddles when I'm telling the story, just for fun!

69